The Bear and the Wildcat

Written by Kazumi Yumoto and illustrated by Komako Sakai

Translated by Cathy Hirano

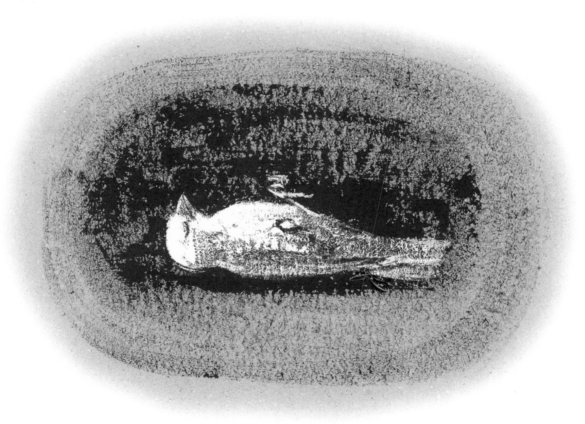

GECKO PRESS

One morning, Bear was crying.

His best friend, a little bird, was dead.

Bear cut a tree from the forest and made a little box.
He stained it with berry juice and lined it with petals.
Then he gently laid his friend inside.

The little bird looked as if he was only sleeping.
His downy feathers were the colour of coral and his
tiny black beak gleamed like onyx.

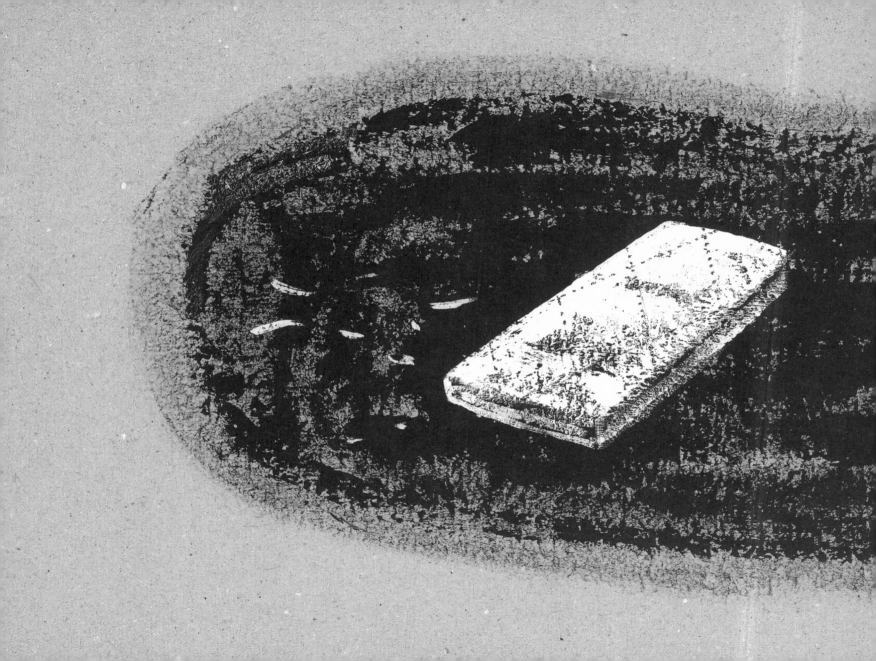

Bear thought back to the morning before.

"Little bird," he had said. "Today it is this morning, isn't it? Yesterday and the day before yesterday it was 'this morning,' too. Isn't that strange? Morning will come again tomorrow and the day after tomorrow, but it will still be 'this morning.' It's always this morning and we're always together, aren't we?"

The little bird had cocked his head and said, "Yes, Bear. But you know what? More than yesterday morning or tomorrow morning, I like this morning best of all."

And now he was gone.

"Yesterday I had no idea that today you would be dead!"
Bear cried. "If only I could go back to yesterday
morning, I wouldn't need anything else in the world."
Big tears rolled down his face.

After that, Bear took the box with him wherever he went.
All the animals he met said, "What a beautiful box!
What's inside?"

But when he showed them, they frowned and fell silent.

They always said, "He'll never come back to life, Bear.
It may be hard, but you have to forget about him."

Bear went home and locked the door.

Day and night, he sat in the dark, shut up in his room.

Sometimes sleep took hold of him. He would doze off,
still sitting in his chair.

Then, one day, Bear opened the window...and found the sun shining!

The breeze was scented with grass. He went outside and looked up at the sky and the clouds sailing by, as if seeing them for the first time.

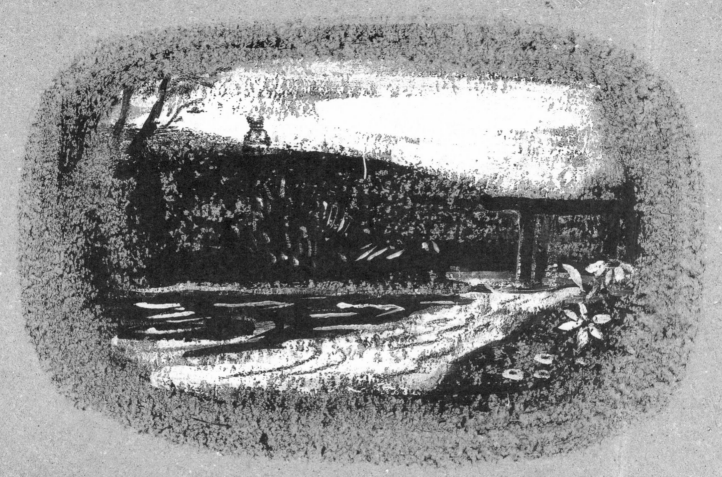

Bear began to walk. He walked through the forest and along the riverbank. The grass was a rich green and the water glistened.

He came upon a strange wildcat napping on the bank.
On the grass beside him lay a tattered knapsack and
an odd-shaped box.

Bear had to see what was inside it.

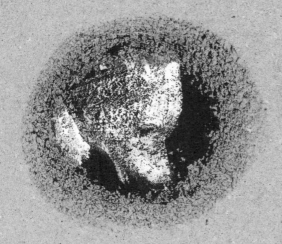

"I..." he began, but it sounded like a croak because he had not spoken for so long.

The wildcat opened one eye and said, "Do you want something?"

"I'd like to see what's in your box,"
Bear said, his voice catching.
The wildcat opened both eyes.
"All right," he said. "I'll show you..."

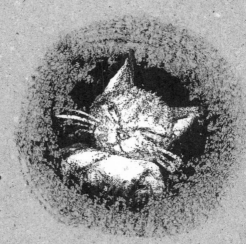

"…as long as you show me what's inside that pretty box of yours."

Bear hesitated, but then he opened it. The little bird lay
peacefully on the bed of fragrant petals. The wildcat looked
at him for a long time. Then he raised his head.

"This little bird must have been a very special friend of yours,"
he said. "You must miss him a lot."
Bear looked up in surprise. No one had ever said that before.

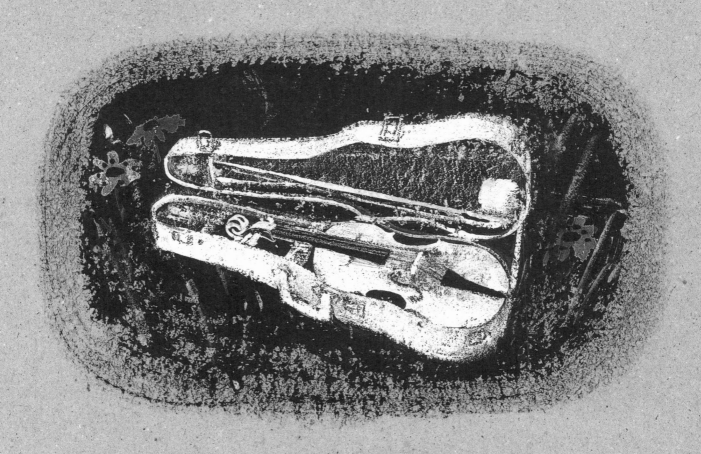

The wildcat opened his box. Inside was a violin.
He took it out and said, "Let me play a song for you
and your little friend."

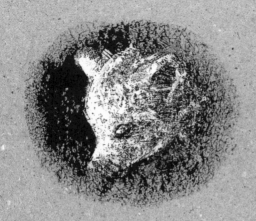

Bear closed his eyes and listened
to the wildcat play.

Memories came flooding back.
Once, a weasel had attacked the little bird.
Bear had stayed up night after night to nurse
him. The little bird never complained, but he
was sad and embarrassed because the weasel
had pulled out all his tail feathers.

Quietly, the violin played on.

Bear had collected pretty leaves for his
friend and tied them on his tail. It made
the little bird very happy. Bear could still
see him strutting in circles trying to see
the bright leaves behind him.

The memory made Bear smile.

Bear thought back over their special times together.
He remembered how the tiny black beak had tickled when
the bird pecked Bear's forehead to wake him each morning.
How the little bird always beat him at counting berries,
no matter how fast Bear counted.

How they bathed together on sunny days at the spring in the
forest. The little bird always complained when Bear splashed.
He remembered the smell of the bird's wet feathers after the bath.
He remembered the times they fought and how they always made
up again. Bear remembered everything.

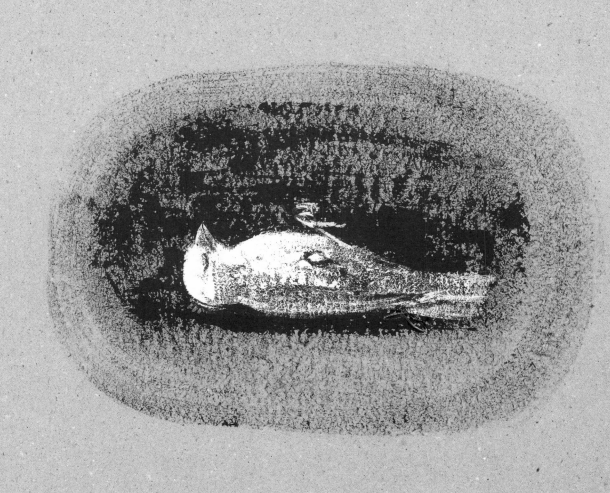

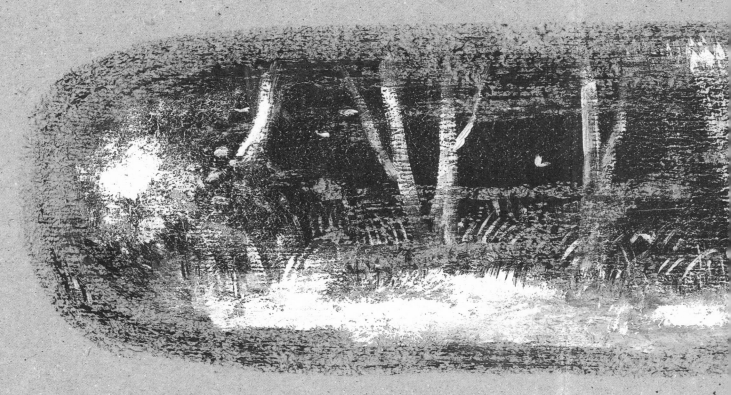

In the middle of the forest was a clearing where
the sun shone and the two had often played.
This was where Bear buried his friend. "I won't
be sad anymore," he said, "because we'll always
be friends, my little bird and I."

The wildcat found a pretty stone, about the size
of the little bird. He placed it on top, and he and
Bear decorated the spot with flowers.

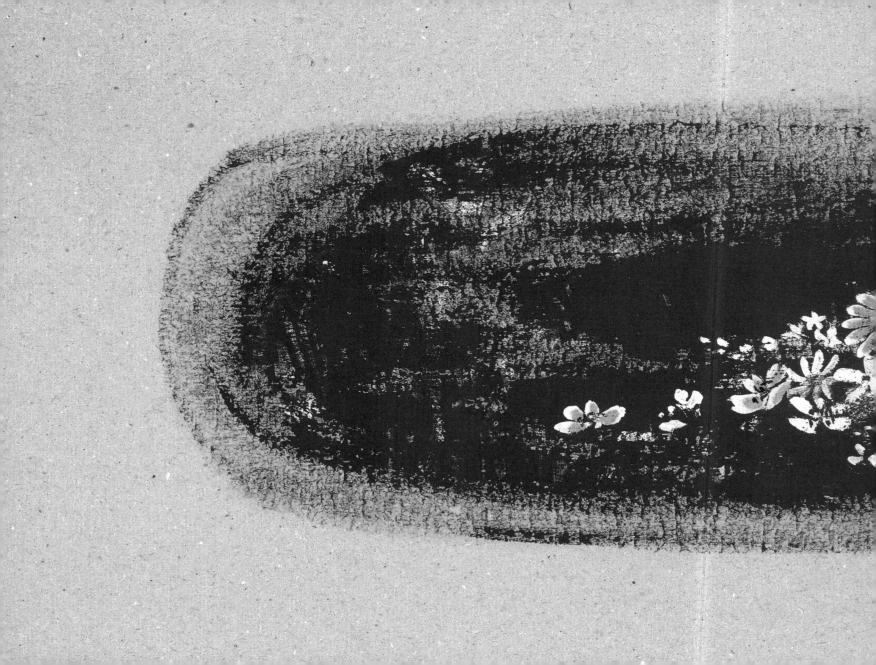

The wildcat looked up at the sky. "I guess it's time to go," he said.

"Where are you going?" Bear asked.

"Wherever I feel like," the wildcat answered as he picked up his violin case.

"I travel from one town to the next, playing my violin. That's my job. Do you want to come?"

"Me? Go with you?" Bear had never left home in his life. He couldn't play the violin. Yet he liked the idea of visiting unknown places.

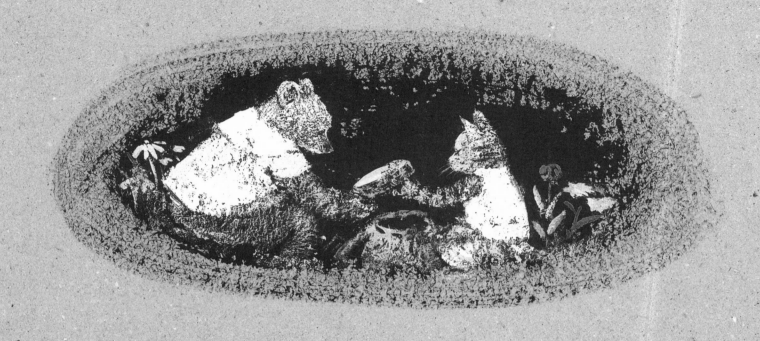

"Come with me, Bear," the wildcat said, and from his tattered
knapsack he took a tambourine. "Here, try playing this."
Bear tapped it gently. It made a lovely sound, like drops
of water falling from leaves in the forest after rain.
Baran, bararararan ...

But what an old tambourine! It was dirty and brown
and covered with paw prints.
Who used to play it? Bear wondered. Had the wildcat
once had a best friend, too?
He wanted to ask, but instead he said:

"I'll try it. Maybe I can even learn to dance and play at the same time."

They have been together ever since.
The Bear and Wildcat Band is very popular wherever it goes.
They are still touring the world so, who knows—maybe one day
they'll come to your town.

First American edition published in 2023.

This edition first published in 2011 by Gecko Press
PO Box 9335, Wellington 6141, Aotearoa New Zealand
office@geckopress.com

English-language edition © Gecko Press Ltd 2011
Translation © Cathy Hirano

Original title: Kuma to Yamaneko
Text © 2008 by Kazumi YUMOTO
Illustrations © 2008 by Komako SAKAI

First published in Japan in 2008 by Kawade Shobo
Shinsha Publishers
English-language translation rights arranged with Kawade Shobo
Shinsha Publishers through Japan Foreign-Rights Centre

A catalogue record for this book is available from the
National Library of New Zealand.

Edited by Penelope Todd
Typesetting by Spencer Levine, New Zealand
Printed by Everbest, China

ISBN hardback: 9781877467707

For more curiously good books, visit www.geckopress.com